I'm Tired, But It's Not Just That

A novel about motherhood, grief, and finally
taking up space

Jalisa Shrader

Dedication

For the mothers who keep going even when no one is clapping.
For the women who were told they were strong when they were actually exhausted.
For the ones learning that rest is not a reward and boundaries are not a betrayal.

For Anthony, Demarcus, Markai, Divinity, Ja'Marr, and for Markelle And Siah.
Still here, in every way that matters.

Acknowledgments

This book was written in the in-between moments. After bedtime. Before the house woke up. In the quiet when everything finally slowed down just enough for me to hear myself think. Because of that, this book belongs to more people than just me.

To my children, all of you, thank you for being my why. For the noise, the chaos, the love, and the patience you didn't even realize you were showing. You gave me purpose on days when I felt lost and reminded me who I needed to be even when I was exhausted.

To Nevaeh, my youngest sister and my first heartbeat, you make resilience, confidence, and bravery look easy. Watching you move through the world has reminded me how powerful it is to be yourself without shrinking. I carry that with me more than you know.

To Siah, you are still with us. In the pauses. In the softness. In the way I love deeper and slower now. You are carried in this book the same way you are carried in my heart, quietly and always.

To Kayla, my person, thank you for being my constant through every stage of motherhood. For the late-night talks, the honesty, the laughter, and the moments you held me up when I couldn't do it myself. I don't know what this journey would have looked like without you, and I am endlessly grateful I never had to find out.

To the mothers who will read these pages and feel seen, especially the ones who are tired and know it is not just that, this book was written for you. You are not weak. You are not invisible. And you are allowed to take up space in your own life.

To the people who showed up without needing explanations, who listened without trying to fix, thank you for giving me room to be honest and unfinished.

And finally, to myself, the version of me who kept going even when disappearing felt easier, this is proof that you survived. And that you learned you did not have to do it quietly anymore.

Chapter One

I'm Tired, But It's Not Just That

Danielle woke up before her alarm, which wasn't discipline so much as conditioning. Her body knew that if she didn't get up first, the day would take that personally.

It was 4:19 a.m. The house was quiet in that fragile, borrowed way that only exists before anyone needs you. No doors slamming. No voices calling her name from different rooms like a group project she never signed up for.

She stood in the kitchen holding a mug that said *World's Best Mom*, which felt less like praise and more like an expectation that never expired. The coffee was already lukewarm. She drank it anyway.

Danielle had six children. Five living. One who changed everything.

Aiden, thirteen, needed structure and predictability in a world that rarely slowed down. Cole, eight, noticed everything and asked for nothing. Kaide, six and a half, listened more than he spoke and was often misunderstood because of it. Nevaeh, five, said whatever came to mind and somehow managed to be both hilarious and exhausting. Chase, four, was all big feelings and louder opinions. And Siah, four months old when he passed the previous summer, existed everywhere and nowhere at once.

Grief didn't announce itself. It didn't collapse her onto the floor or demand her attention every minute. Most days it looked like hesitation. Like counting heads even when everyone was already there. Like knowing exactly how old he would be if he were still here.

Danielle ran through the day in her head like she always did. Drop-offs. Work. Pickups. Dinner. Homework she barely remembered learning herself. Appointments. Bills. The mental math never stopped. It just changed subjects.

People told her she was strong. She heard it often, usually right before someone asked her for something.

She used to think strength meant she was doing something right. Lately, it felt more like proof she hadn't asked for help in a long time.

She wasn't unhappy. That was the confusing part. She loved her kids. She liked her job well enough. She was proud of what she managed with what she had.

But "fine" had started to feel like a ceiling.

She didn't want a vacation. She didn't want a break. She wanted her life to feel lighter. Not easier. Just lighter.

Danielle glanced at the clock. The quiet was almost over.

Before she turned the day back on, she stood there one extra second and let the thought surface fully.

I can't keep doing this the same way.

It didn't feel dramatic. It felt honest.

Chapter Two

This Is Not Burnout

People loved to call it burnout.

Danielle heard it from coworkers, from acquaintances, from strangers who learned just enough about her life to nod sympathetically before offering advice she didn't ask for.

"Sounds like burnout."
"You need to rest."
"You should take a break."

Burnout implied something temporary. Like if she just stepped away long enough, everything would reset and return to normal.

But this wasn't that.

This was years of being the default. Years of being the one who remembered everything, scheduled everything, noticed everything. Years of being the safety net and the backup plan and the emotional regulator.

Burnout was a buzzword people used when they didn't want to look too closely at the system causing the exhaustion.

Danielle wasn't burnt out. She was under-supported.

She could rest for a weekend and still wake up Monday carrying the same mental load. She could sleep for ten hours and still feel tired because tired lived deeper than her bones.

People talked about self-care like it was a cure. A bath. A walk. A glass of wine.

None of those fixed the fact that she was responsible for too much with too little margin.

Calling it burnout made it sound like her fault. Like she just hadn't managed herself properly.

Danielle knew better.

Chapter Three

Six Kids, Five Beds, One Missing

The house had five beds for children and one that stayed empty.

Danielle didn't talk about it much. Not because it hurt too badly, but because explaining grief felt like trying to describe a color people hadn't seen.

Siah had been here for four months. Long enough to be real. Long enough to change everything. Not long enough for the world to know what to do with his absence.

People assumed grief was loud. That it demanded tears and anniversaries and visible breakdowns.

Danielle's grief was quiet. It showed up when she folded laundry and hesitated over clothes she couldn't give away. When she caught herself planning around a baby that wasn't there anymore.

She didn't fall apart. She adjusted.

Grief moved in beside motherhood and stayed.

Chapter Four

Aiden Needs the World to Slow Down

Aiden was thirteen and already tired of a world that refused to meet him halfway.

Sounds lingered too long. Schedules mattered. Changes felt bigger than people understood. Danielle had learned to read his cues before he could always name them himself.

She advocated constantly. At school. At appointments. In rooms where people smiled politely and assumed they knew better.

She softened her voice out of habit, even when she shouldn't have had to.

Aiden wasn't broken. The system just wasn't built for him.

Some days she was exhausted by the explaining. Other days she was in awe of how clearly he saw things everyone else complicated.

Loving Aiden taught Danielle how much work it took to exist in a world that didn't listen.

Chapter Five

Cole Never Asks for Anything

Cole was eight and wise in ways that worried Danielle if she thought about it too long.

He noticed when she was overwhelmed and adjusted himself accordingly. Fewer needs. Quieter presence. Help offered before it was requested.

He tied shoes. Cleared plates. Watched his siblings with the seriousness of someone twice his age.

Danielle leaned on him without meaning to. Because he made it easy. Because he didn't complain. Because he seemed fine.

One night, as she watched him fall asleep clutching a book he pretended not to care about, the thought landed heavier than she expected.

He's still a baby.

Not in the literal sense, but in the way children deserved to be protected from responsibility they never asked for.

Danielle made a mental note to choose him more loudly. To see him before he learned how to disappear.

She didn't know yet how much that choice would matter.

Chapter Six

Kaide Is Listening Even When You're Not

Kaide was six and a half and understood far more than people gave him credit for.

He listened first. Always. He watched conversations happen before stepping into them, like he was waiting to be sure his timing wouldn't bother anyone. When he did speak, it was careful. Measured. And often interrupted.

His speech came slower than his thoughts, and Danielle could see the gap widen every time someone finished his sentence for him or moved on too quickly. She noticed how his eyes followed conversations even after people assumed he'd checked out.

He hadn't.

Kaide absorbed everything. Tone. Mood. Tension. He stored it quietly and made sense of it later, usually when no one was looking.

Danielle tried to slow things down for him. Tried to make space. But life moved fast, and Kaide learned early how to move with it instead of against it.

Sometimes, late at night, he would say something so perceptive it stopped her cold. A question. An observation. A truth that made her wonder how often she missed him during the noise of the day.

She promised herself she would listen harder.

Chapter Seven

Nevaeh Says What Everyone's Thinking

Nevaeh was five and had never met a thought she didn't think deserved airtime.

She was bold in a house full of boys, bossy without apology, and already fluent in sarcasm she definitely learned at home. She asked questions that made adults laugh and then wince, sometimes in the same breath.

Danielle loved her confidence. She just struggled with the edges of it.

Teaching Nevaeh kindness without shrinking her felt like walking a line Danielle herself had fallen off years ago. She didn't want her daughter to be quiet. She wanted her to be thoughtful. There was a difference, even if the world pretended there wasn't.

Nevaeh challenged her constantly. Not out of defiance, but curiosity. She wanted to know why rules existed and who decided them. She wanted explanations that made sense.

Some days Danielle felt like she was parenting a mirror. Other days, a warning.

Chapter Eight

Chase and the Myth of Hot Coffee

Chase was four and believed patience was optional.

He entered rooms loudly and emotionally, like he had somewhere important to be and no interest in waiting. His laughter filled the house. His tantrums did too.

Danielle joked that Chase was the reason her coffee never stayed hot. Not because he spilled it, but because he needed something every time she tried to sit down.

He wanted attention immediately and fully, and Danielle gave it more often than she should have because it felt easier than negotiating with a four-year-old who had opinions and volume.

Chase was joy and exhaustion bundled into one small body. He reminded her that chaos didn't always mean something was wrong.

Sometimes it just meant someone was alive and unapologetic about it.

Chapter Nine

Grief Doesn't Announce Itself

Grief didn't come with warning signs or schedules.

It slipped into ordinary moments. The grocery store. The car. The space between breaths when everything else was quiet.

Danielle didn't cry every day. That surprised people. It surprised her too, at first.

Instead, she carried it. In her chest. In her habits. In the way she loved her children with an urgency she didn't explain.

Siah's absence was constant, but it wasn't always loud. Some days it was just a thought she didn't finish. A pause she didn't explain.

Grief didn't ask permission. It simply lived alongside everything else.

Chapter Ten

Why "Help" Is Never What It Sounds Like

People offered help all the time.

"Let me know if you need anything."
"Just ask."
"I'm here."

Danielle learned quickly that most of those offers still required her to manage the work. To ask. To plan. To explain. To follow up.

Help often came with conditions. With opinions. With reminders of how much easier things would be if she did things differently.

She started noticing how often help still centered her effort. How rarely it actually reduced her load.

Danielle didn't need more advice. She needed less responsibility.

That realization settled quietly but firmly. Another crack in the way things had always been done.

Chapter Eleven

The Math Is Always Running

Danielle did math constantly, even when no numbers were involved.

Time math. Money math. Emotional math. The kind that never made it onto paper but lived permanently in her head.

If she left five minutes late, everything else shifted. If one bill was higher than expected, three other things had to shrink. If one child needed more, another would need to wait. She balanced it all instinctively, like someone who had been doing it long enough to forget it wasn't normal.

People assumed she was organized. Efficient. On top of things.

What they didn't see was how tired that kind of awareness made her. How her brain never truly rested because it was always tracking something. Someone. Some future problem she could prevent if she stayed alert enough.

She couldn't remember the last time she'd been fully present without calculating what came next.

The math was always running.

Chapter Twelve

You're So Strong

People said it like a compliment.

"You're so strong."
"I don't know how you do it."
"I could never handle all that."

Danielle smiled politely every time, even though the words landed heavier than people realized.

Strong was what they called her when they didn't plan to step in. When they noticed the weight but decided admiration was easier than action.

Strength sounded flattering until it started to feel like a role she couldn't step out of without disappointing someone.

No one asked if she wanted to be strong. They just assumed she'd keep going.

Danielle wondered what would happen if she stopped performing resilience and started telling the truth.

Chapter Thirteen

Middle Child Syndrome Is Real

Kaide sat quietly while his siblings talked over one another.

Not because he didn't have anything to say, but because he was used to waiting for space that didn't always come.

Danielle watched him from across the room and felt a familiar tug of guilt. He wasn't the loudest. He wasn't the one teachers flagged or praised first. He didn't demand attention.

He slipped through the cracks simply by being easy.

Middle child syndrome sounded like a joke until she saw it playing out in real time. Until she noticed how often Kaide's needs were assumed instead of asked about.

She made a promise, right there, to interrupt the noise for him when she needed to. To slow the room down. To make space where none existed.

Chapter Fourteen

The Day She Realizes Cole Is Still a Baby

It happened on an ordinary night.

Cole was brushing his teeth, methodical and quiet, when Danielle realized she hadn't checked on him emotionally in days. Not really. She relied on his competence. His calm. His ability to manage himself.

She watched him climb into bed and suddenly saw him differently. Not as the helper. Not as the easy one.

As a child.

A child who deserved attention that wasn't earned through usefulness.

The realization hit her harder than she expected.

Danielle sat beside him longer than usual that night, listening to him talk about things he rarely brought up. She let herself feel the weight of how often she'd mistaken maturity for readiness.

She made another promise. This one louder.

Chapter Fifteen

Advocating Without Apologizing

Danielle noticed it first in her voice.

How she softened it. Lowered it. Smoothed the edges before speaking up. Especially in rooms where authority lived.

She apologized before making requests. Added qualifiers. Explained herself more than necessary.

One day, mid-sentence, she stopped.

She stated what Aiden needed without cushioning it. Without justification. Without apology.

The room shifted. People looked uncomfortable.

Danielle didn't.

Advocating without apologizing felt strange at first. Like she was breaking an unspoken rule. But the more she practiced it, the more natural it became.

She wasn't asking for special treatment. She was asking for basic consideration.

And she was done pretending that required permission.

Chapter Sixteen

Being the Default Parent Isn't a Personality Trait

Danielle didn't remember when it happened exactly. There wasn't a meeting or a conversation where roles were assigned.

She just became the one.

The one who remembered birthdays and dentist appointments. The one who noticed when shoes were too small or moods were off. The one who knew everyone's schedules without checking a calendar.

Being the default parent looked like competence from the outside. On the inside, it felt like carrying a running list that never shut off.

People praised her for it. Told her she was amazing. Organized. On top of things.

None of that made it lighter.

Danielle realized she had confused responsibility with identity. Somewhere along the way, being the default became who she was instead of something she did.

And that realization sat with her longer than she expected.

Chapter Seventeen

Nevaeh Learns the Word No

Nevaeh did not take no personally. She took it as a challenge.

Danielle watched her daughter push boundaries with the confidence of someone who knew she was loved no matter what. That confidence both impressed her and exhausted her.

Saying no felt harder with Nevaeh than with the boys. Danielle worried about dampening her spark. About teaching her to be smaller.

But she was starting to understand that boundaries didn't erase confidence. They shaped it.

Nevaeh tested her anyway. Pouted. Negotiated. Said things that made Danielle bite her tongue to keep from laughing.

Eventually, Nevaeh accepted it and moved on.

Danielle noticed something then. The no didn't damage their relationship. It strengthened it.

Chapter Eighteen

When Grief Meets Exhaustion

Danielle hadn't rested since Siah.

Not really.

She had slept. She had gone through the motions. She had kept everything running. But rest implied safety, and her body hadn't felt safe enough to let go.

Grief had rewired her nervous system. Every sound felt louder. Every silence heavier.

She realized she had been surviving instead of living, not because she wanted to, but because it felt necessary.

Exhaustion wasn't just physical. It was the weight of never letting her guard down.

Naming that didn't fix it, but it gave it shape. And that mattered.

Chapter Nineteen

Danielle Stops Explaining Herself

It started small.

She declined an invitation without offering an excuse. She set a boundary without cushioning it with guilt.

People noticed.

Questions followed. Confusion. A few raised eyebrows.

Danielle held steady.

Explaining herself had always felt like a reflex. Like proof she wasn't being unreasonable. Letting go of that felt risky, but also freeing.

She realized how much energy she had spent managing other people's reactions to her needs.

She stopped.

Chapter Twenty

Rest Is Not a Reward

Danielle had treated rest like something that had to be earned.

Finish the work. Take care of everyone else. Prove you deserve it.

She started to question that logic.

Rest wasn't a prize for endurance. It was a requirement for being human.

She rested even when things weren't perfect. Even when the list wasn't finished.

Nothing bad happened.

The world kept turning. The kids adjusted. The guilt softened.

Danielle realized that rest didn't make her less capable.

It made her clearer.

Chapter Twenty-One

What Happens When She Doesn't Say Yes

The first thing Danielle noticed was the silence.

Not the peaceful kind. The kind that lingered a second too long after she declined something she would have automatically agreed to before.

She didn't fill it.

She waited.

People stumbled over their responses. Some laughed awkwardly. Others looked confused, like they were trying to recalibrate an expectation they hadn't realized they had.

Danielle felt it in her chest, that old urge to explain herself. To soften the no. To make it more comfortable for everyone else.

She didn't.

The moment passed. Slightly uncomfortable. Entirely survivable.

She realized then how much of her energy had gone into preventing other people from feeling mild disappointment.

Chapter Twenty-Two

The Guilt Tries One Last Time

Guilt didn't disappear quietly.

It showed up late at night, when the house was finally still. When Danielle replayed conversations and wondered if she had been too much. Too firm. Too distant.

It tried to convince her that she was being selfish. That she was failing some invisible test of goodness she had been unknowingly taking her entire life.

She almost listened.

Almost apologized. Almost backtracked.

But then she noticed something new.

She felt calmer.

Not happier exactly. Just steadier. Less frayed.

Danielle realized guilt was loudest when it was losing control.

Chapter Twenty-Three

Boundaries Make People Loud

The pushback came eventually.

Not everyone liked the new version of Danielle. Some missed how easy she used to be. How flexible. How accommodating.

They asked pointed questions. Made comments disguised as concern.

"You've changed."
"You don't seem like yourself."
"Is everything okay?"

Danielle heard what they were really asking.

Why aren't you doing what you used to do?

She answered simply. "I'm good."

And let them sit with their discomfort.

Chapter Twenty-Four

Danielle Chooses Herself

Choosing herself didn't look dramatic.

It looked like protecting her time. Delegating without guilt. Letting things stay unfinished without panicking.

It looked like saying yes only when she meant it.

She didn't burn bridges. She just stopped crossing them alone.

The surprising part was how much room that created. Not just in her schedule, but in her mind.

Danielle felt herself settling into her own life for the first time in years.

Chapter Twenty-Five

Cole Notices

Cole was the first to say something.

They were sitting together quietly when he looked up at her and asked, "Are you happier?"

The question caught her off guard.

She thought about it. About tiredness that didn't crush her the same way. About space she hadn't known she needed.

"I think I'm more here," she said.

Cole nodded, like that was the right answer.

Danielle realized then that choosing herself wasn't something her children had to recover from.

It was something they could learn from.

Chapter Twenty-Six

Aiden Tells the Truth No One Else Will

Aiden noticed before anyone else said anything out loud.

"You're not rushing anymore," he said one afternoon, like it was a fact he'd been collecting quietly.

Danielle paused. "Is that bad?"

He shook his head. "No. It's better. People listen more when you don't rush."

She smiled, because of course he would notice that. Of course he would name it so plainly.

Aiden had always seen the world clearly. He just lived in a system that made clarity inconvenient.

Danielle realized then that slowing down hadn't just helped her. It had given him room too.

Chapter Twenty-Seven

Kaide Finally Gets Heard

Kaide spoke when the room was quiet.

Not because Danielle told him to, but because she waited.

She noticed how his words came carefully, how his thoughts arrived fully formed once he had space to finish them. She watched others lean in instead of rushing ahead.

Later that night, he crawled into her lap and said, "I like when you wait."

Danielle held him tighter than necessary.

She wondered how many moments like that she'd missed before she learned how to stop moving so fast.

Chapter Twenty-Eight

The Thing She's Been Avoiding

There was one conversation Danielle had been circling for months.

Not because she didn't know what to say, but because she knew saying it would change things.

She sat with the discomfort instead of running from it. Let herself imagine the fallout. The questions. The resistance.

And then she imagined staying the same.

That was worse.

Chapter Twenty-Nine

She Says It Out Loud

Her voice didn't shake.

That surprised her most of all.

She said what she needed. What she would no longer carry alone. What she was no longer available for.

There was silence after.

Danielle didn't rush to fill it.

She let the truth stand on its own.

Chapter Thirty

This Is What Changes

Not everything shifted immediately.

Some things stayed hard. Some people stayed uncomfortable.

But Danielle felt something settle inside her. Like she'd finally stopped bracing for impact that never came.

The world didn't collapse.

Her life didn't fall apart.

It adjusted.

Chapter Thirty-One

Not Less of a Mother

Danielle worried, briefly, that choosing herself would make her less patient. Less present. Less loving.

It did the opposite.

She listened more. Laughed more. Snapped less.

Her children didn't lose her.

They gained her.

Chapter Thirty-Two

Still Grieving, Still Standing

Grief remained.

It always would.

But it no longer owned every quiet moment. It existed alongside joy now, not instead of it.

Danielle stopped measuring healing by the absence of pain.

She measured it by how fully she could live with it.

Chapter Thirty-Three

The Kids Adjust

Children, Danielle learned, were incredibly adaptable when the adults stopped carrying everything for them.

They stepped up. Softened. Grew.

They didn't need her to disappear.

They needed her to stay.

Chapter Thirty-Four

She Takes Up Space

Danielle no longer apologized for existing loudly in her own life.

She took breaks. Set limits. Let herself be seen.

The world adjusted around her instead of the other way around.

She realized she hadn't been asking for too much before.

She had been asking the wrong people.

Chapter Thirty-Five

It Was Never Just Tired

Danielle didn't wake up different the morning it finally felt complete.

The house still moved the same way. The kids still needed her. Grief still lived quietly alongside everything else.

But Danielle no longer disappeared to make it all work.

She stopped explaining herself. Stopped shrinking. Stopped treating rest like a reward.

She was a good mother.

And a whole person.

Those things never competed.

It had never been just tired.

It had been time.

About the Author

Jalisa Shrader is a millennial mother and writer whose work explores motherhood, grief, neurodivergent parenting, and the invisible labor women carry every day. She writes emotionally honest fiction for readers who have been told they are "so strong" when what they really needed was support.

Her debut novel, *I'm Tired, But It's Not Just That*, is a quiet, powerful story about a woman who stops shrinking to make everything work and begins taking up space without apology. Jalisa's writing is reflective, grounded, and occasionally humorous, shaped by lived experience and a deep understanding of what it means to carry responsibility silently.

Jalisa writes in the in-between moments, after bedtime and before the day begins, and lives with her children. When she is not writing, she is navigating motherhood, listening closely, and learning to rest without guilt.

Made in the USA
Middletown, DE
06 February 2026

28171089R00031